I Want My Tent!

Licensed by The Illuminated Film Company
Based on the LITTLE PRINCESS animation series © The Illuminated Film Company 2007
Made under licence by Andersen Press Ltd., London
'I Want My Tent!' episode written by Kelly Marshall
Producer Iain Harvey.   Director Edward Foster
© The Illuminated Film Company/Tony Ross 2007
Design and layout © Andersen Press Ltd., 2007.
Printed and bound in China by C&C Offset Printing.
10   9   8   7   6   5   4   3   2   1
British Library Cataloguing in Publication Data available.

ISBN: 978 1 84270 656 5 (Trade edition)
ISBN: 978 1 84939 699 8 (Riverside Books edition)

I Want My Tent!

Tony Ross

Andersen Press · London

Gilbert sat quietly while the Little Princess read him a story. She was hosting a tea party in her brand new washing-line tent.

"I made it all by myself," she grinned proudly. Suddenly there was a loud shriek outside.

"My sheets!"

The Maid stuck her head in.
"Sorry, Princess, but you
can't play with my sheets.
I have lots of royal beds to make."
The tent was unpegged and folded up in seconds.

"You've ruined my game!"

gasped the Little Princess.

"Maybe you could play something else?" replied the Maid.

But the Little Princess only wanted to play camping.

The Little Princess loaded Gilbert and all the toys back into her pram.

"I'll make another tent," she decided, "better than that silly old sheet."

She marched through the garden until she spotted the right place.

"Hmmm… maybe."

The Little Princess crawled under the
table and sat down. It wasn't much fun.
"No," she frowned. "My tent has to be special."

As she walked across the lawn, the Little Princess spotted the King's croquet mallets.
"I could use those to make another tent!"
The Little Princess worked hard. She carefully held all the mallets together, tying them in place with a skipping rope.

When she threw her blanket over the top it turned into...

an incredible
purple
tepee!

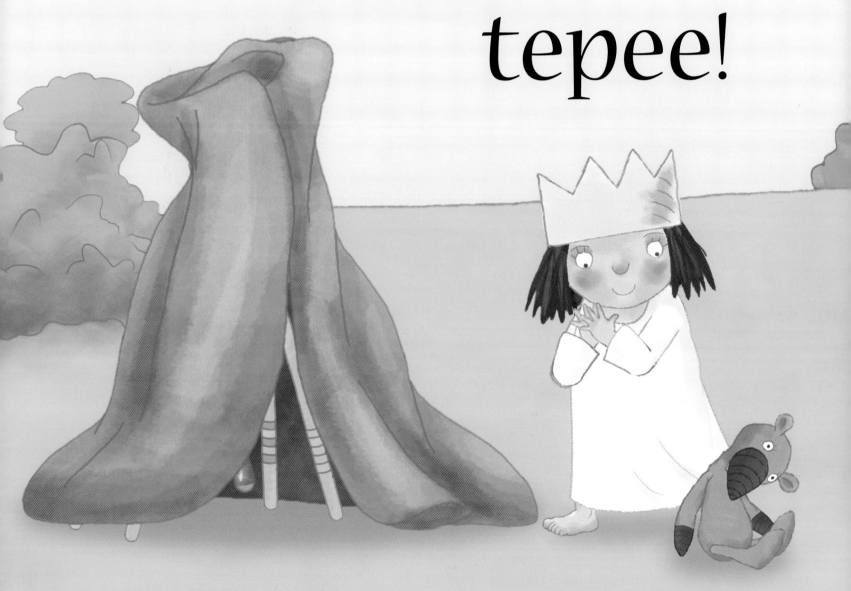

The Little Princess cuddled Gilbert inside their cosy new tent.

"Now we can play proper camping!" she giggled.

"Princess have you seen my croquet mallets?"

The King's head peeped through a gap in the blanket.

The Little Princess sighed.

"I'm afraid I need them for an important game,"

the King explained, as he carried them away.

The Little Princess's lovely new tent collapsed.

The Little Princess stomped up to her bedroom.

"It's not fair," she muttered. "Everyone keeps spoiling my game."

She stood on tiptoe and gazed out of the window.

"I need to find somewhere nice and quiet."

A bluebird fluttered past, gliding down to a nest on the branch of a tree.

The Little Princess grinned from ear to ear.

"That's it!"

The Little Princess threw her purple blanket over the branch,
then stood back to admire it.

"Something's missing," she decided.

Luckily the garden was full of things to brighten up the tent.

She found a gnome near the Admiral's pond and all sorts of treasures near the greenhouse.

"A plant, a watering can and these!" smiled the Little Princess, picking up the Gardener's wellington boots.

The Little Princess thought that the outside of the tent looked just right.

"Now to make it a real home," she whispered.

First stop was the kitchen.

"Can I have some milk and biscuits to eat in my tent?" asked the Little Princess.

"*Oui. Oui.* But only one," said the Chef, trying to ice his cake. "Now shoo, shoo, shoo!"

The Little Princess burst into the Queen's parlour.

"Can I have some of your wool for my tent?"

Her mother smiled at the King. "Of course, dear."

"I'm going to live in my tent for ever!" announced the Little Princess, running back out to the garden.

By the time she'd loaded up the pram with everything she needed, it was quite a job to push it back to her tent.

"Hold it there!" called the Little Princess.
Scruff and Puss balanced on buckets while she painted
their portraits.
"I just need some nice pictures and my tent will feel like home,"
the Little Princess smiled.

The paintings were pegged up in no time.
The Little Princess was so pleased with
her comfy new tent, she decided to
have a tea party.
Nobody noticed two curious mice
creeping in.

"Biscuit anyone?" asked the Little Princess in a grown-up voice. She proudly lifted up the bucket that was keeping her biscuit plate fresh.
The Little Princess gasped. "Mices!"

The two brown mice trembled amongst the crumbs and scampered away.
Suddenly there was a clap of thunder. Rain started to pour through the tent, onto the Little Princess's head. All of her lovely paintings were ruined!

"Much better," soothed the Maid ten minutes later. "All nice and warm."

"But my tent is all soggy," cried the Little Princess.

The Maid wrapped the fluffy bath towel more snugly around her. "I'll dry it out tonight."

Before she could argue, the Little Princess
found herself tucked up in bed.
"I'll tell the Queen you're ready for your
goodnight kiss," smiled the Maid.
The Little Princess dived under the covers.
"Gilbert, where are you?"

The Little Princess knew exactly
where to find Gilbert. She crept
down the castle staircase and then
made a dash for the castle laundry.

"Shhhh!"

Scruff and Puss jumped out of their basket and padded
silently behind her.
"Gilbert!" cried the Little Princess, pushing open the laundry
door. "Aha!"
There was teddy Gilbert hanging from a peg, plus all of her
camping things!

"Nighty nighty," said the Queen, when she popped up to the Little Princess's bedroom.

"Princess?" asked the Maid.

They both gasped – the room was empty.

The castle was searched from top to bottom, right down to the royal laundry.

Suddenly, the Queen pointed to the clothes rack.

They could just see the Little Princess curled up inside…

...the best tent ever!